Sandy Lane Stables

Sandy Lane Stables

The Runaway Pony

Susannah Leigh

Adapted by: Katie Daynes

Reading consultant: Alison Kelly

American editor: Carrie Armstrong

Series editor: Lesley Sims

Designed by: Brenda Cole

Cover and inside illustrations: Barbara Bongini

Map illustrations: John Woodcock

This edition first published in 2016 by Usborne Publishing Ltd.,
Usborne House, 83-85 Saffron Hill, London EC1N 8RT, England.
www.usborne.com

Copyright © Usborne Publishing 2016, 2009, 2003, 1997

Illustrations copyright © Usborne Publishing, 2016

A CIP catalogue record for this book is available from the British Library.

Contents

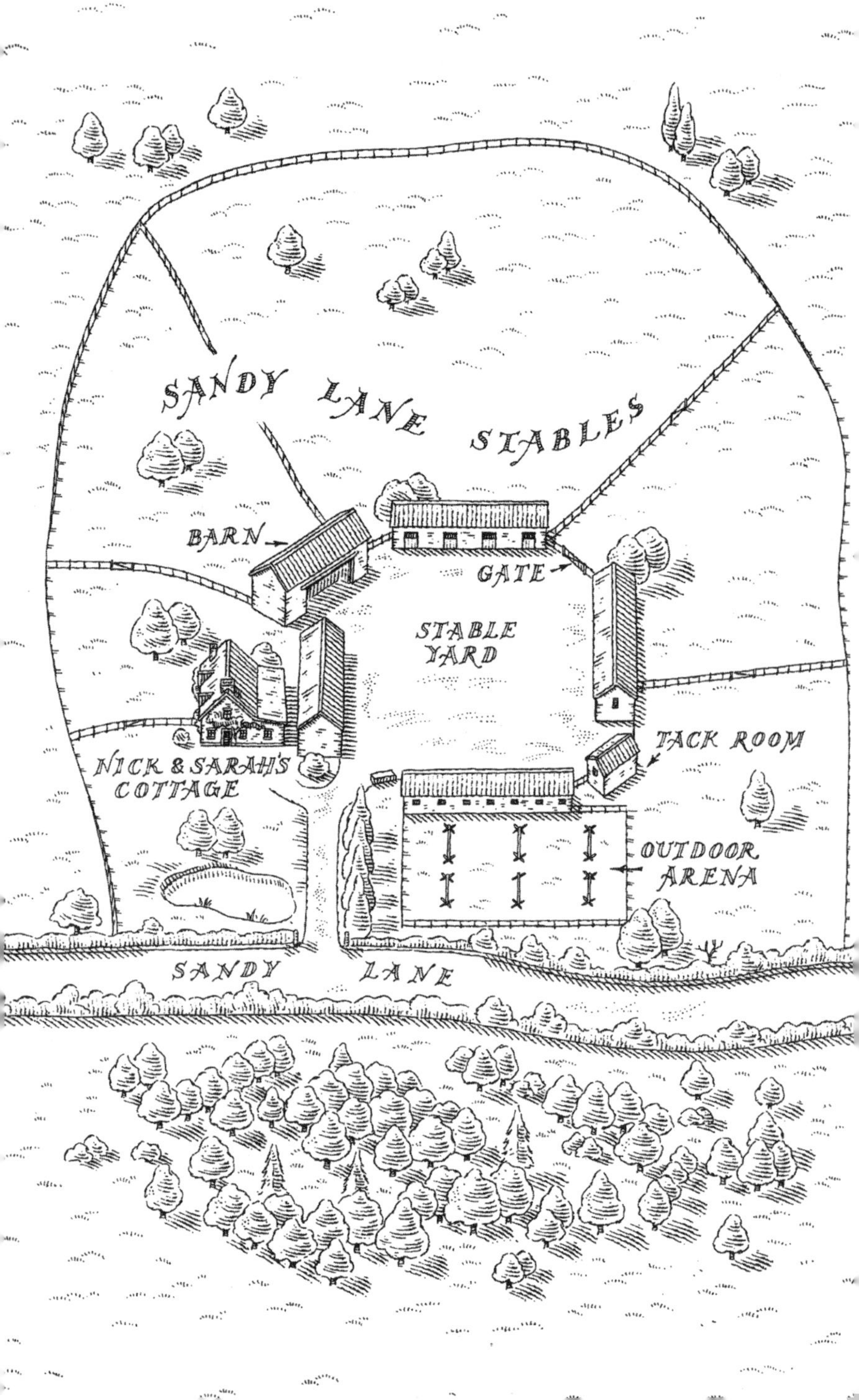

SANDY LANE STABLES

BARN →

← GATE

STABLE YARD

TACK ROOM

NICK & SARAH'S COTTAGE

OUTDOOR ARENA

SANDY LANE

Chapter 1

The Runaway Pony

Jess Adams free-wheeled her bicycle down the country lane. "No more school!" she cheered. "Hurray for the vacation!"

She turned into the driveway of Sandy Lane Stables and skidded the bike to a halt. It was early morning and no one else was around. Only the ponies were awake, whinnying softly for their breakfasts. Jess glanced at the little stone cottage tucked away behind the stables.

"I bet Nick and Sarah won't be up for hours," she said to herself.

Nick and Sarah Brooks were the owners of Sandy Lane. Last night had been a rare evening off. They had gone to a charity gala.

"It's in aid of the Horse Rescue Society," Sarah had said merrily, twirling around the stable yard in her borrowed evening dress.

"I bet you'll be dancing all night," Jess had said.

"Probably," Nick had replied, adjusting his tie.

"And you're bound to be really tired in the morning," Jess had continued, forking the last of the hay into Minstrel's hay net. "So maybe I ought to come in early and start the ponies' breakfasts for you. And then maybe…"

"…you could have a free ride later on in the day?" Nick had finished her sentence with a smile. Money was tight in Jess's family since her dad had lost his job. There wasn't much spare cash for riding lessons.

"You can have the eleven o'clock ride for free," Nick had said in an understanding voice.

That was last night. Now it was morning and Jess was alone with the ponies. She didn't mind. She had been coming to Sandy Lane for two years now and she certainly knew enough to start getting the ponies ready for the day.

"Maybe Nick will even let me ride you this afternoon," she said hopefully as she drew closer to Storm Cloud's stall.

A dappled-gray Arab greeted Jess eagerly, poking her face over the stall door. Jess slipped her the sugar lump she had been saving especially for her. She had never seen a pony so breathtaking.

Jess thought back to the day Nick had bought Storm Cloud at the Ash Hill Horse Sale. The pony had been weak and neglected, but Nick had instantly seen her potential. With love and patience, he had brought her back to her former glory. Storm Cloud was a natural jumper. She'd soon compete again.

In Jess's mind, Storm Cloud was the best pony at the stables. She might look delicate, but she was really gutsy. On the few occasions Jess had been lucky enough to ride her, she had felt invincible. It was Jess's secret dream to jump Storm Cloud in a show and ride off with the championship trophy.

"What a team we'd make, eh, Stormy?" Jess whispered into the pony's ear. Storm Cloud neighed gently in reply. At the same time, Jess heard a whinny from a nearby stall. She grinned as Minstrel, the little skewbald pony, showed his big yellow teeth and rolled his eyes at her.

"Of course I haven't forgotten you." Jess laughed.

Minstrel was Jess's regular pony at Sandy Lane. He was a good, solid riding school pony and Jess was very fond of him.

"I expect I'll be riding you later on, Minstrel," Jess began as she made her way over to the pony's stall. "Bet you can't wait..."

"COME HERE!"

Angry shouting and the crunch of hooves on gravel made Jess spin around sharply. Careering toward her, wild-eyed with fear, was a palomino pony. It was completely out of control. Jess's heart began to pound and her breath came in sharp gasps. Almost without thinking, she held out her arms.

"Whoa, little pony," she said, as calmly as she could. "Slow down."

Jess stood her ground as the pony pounded nearer. At the sound of Jess's voice it clattered to a halt. Dropping its head, it nuzzled a velvety nose into her shoulder. Jess sighed with relief. The next moment she had located a stray mint in her jodhpur pocket. Gingerly she offered it to the palomino. The pony, a pretty little mare of about 14 hands, crunched contentedly. For a brief moment, Jess and the pony stood nose to nose, the white gold of the pony's mane contrasting with Jess's own dark curls.

"Come back, you!"

A stocky man ran into the stable yard. His face was red from shouting and he was panting hard. In his hand he waved a muddy halter. The pony started, but Jess calmed it with her hand.

When the man saw Jess he made an effort to compose himself. "Thanks a lot!" he gasped.

"That's all right," Jess said, trying to sound as if catching a runaway pony wasn't a big deal.

"You were very brave standing your ground like that," the man acknowledged.

Jess shrugged her shoulders in what she hoped was a casual way. She couldn't help stealing a glance at the cottage to see if Nick or Sarah had witnessed her bravery, but there was still no sign of them.

The pony butted her nose against Jess's shoulder.

"She's beautiful" said Jess. "What's her name?"

"Um...Goldie." The man leaned forward and put his hands on his knees, still trying to catch his breath. "Because her coat shimmers like gold."

"She looks as precious as gold, too. Don't you, pretty girl?" Jess turned to the pony again.

"She may look like an angel," the man huffed irritably. "But she's a devil to catch. I was trying to load her into the horse trailer when she took flight..."

"She probably caught scent of the horses here and decided to investigate," said Jess.

"Well, it's a good thing you were here to stop her," he replied. "She's not my pony...she belongs to my daughter –" The man stopped abruptly. "Anyway,

I've got to get her back." He moved swiftly toward the palomino, who started and shied.

"I'm no good with animals," he muttered.

"Here, let me try," said Jess, holding out her hand for the halter. Talking gently and murmuring words of encouragement, she stroked the mare's nose firmly with her left hand while deftly slipping on the halter with her right. Goldie didn't flinch. Taking the lead rein in her hand, Jess turned back to the man, who gave a sigh of relief.

"Nice work," he said. "You've been a real help." He tugged at the lead rein and this time the pony trotted obediently behind.

Jess stood watching, puzzled, as they disappeared out of sight. Where was Goldie kept? she wondered. Why didn't his daughter catch the pony herself?

Minstrel whinnied loudly from his stall, cutting into her thoughts.

"All right boy." Jess dragged her mind away from the palomino. "It's breakfast time. Now, what should it be this morning? Hay, hay...or hay?"

Chapter 2

Nick Has Some News

"Finish up your cereal for goodness' sake, Jess." Her mother looked exasperated as Jess pushed soggy cornflakes around her bowl.

"Sorry, Mom, I was miles away." Jess lifted her head from her hand and yawned loudly. Going to the stables so early without stopping for breakfast had been more tiring than she imagined.

"What time did you leave the house this morning?" her mother asked, shaking her head.

"Six...six thirty," Jess answered nonchalantly.

"And on the first day of the break!" Her brother,

Jack, looked up from his toast with a mixture of disgust and disbelief. "You're nuts, Jess."

Jess's mother sighed and continued her lecture. "You spend far too much time at that stables, Jess. I hope you don't think you'll be down there every day of the break. What about your homework?"

Jess sank down in her chair. She knew it was no good trying to explain how utterly necessary ponies were to her life. Instead she gobbled down the rest of her cereal and bolted for the door.

"I've got a ride at eleven. It's free," she explained hastily, "in return for the work I did this morning."

Her mother accepted defeat. "Oh, Jess...if only you spent as much time on your school work as you did at that stables." She sighed. "Don't be back late."

"I won't," Jess promised. "See you later. Bye!"

Jess grabbed her bicycle from the tiny front yard and sped off. She didn't want to think about school work – not when the sun was shining and there were ponies to ride. Her thoughts turned dreamily to Goldie, the palomino pony that had run into

Sandy Lane that morning.

In her mind she wasn't pedaling along the road to Sandy Lane, but cantering cross-country. As she swung into the stable yard the rusty red bicycle beneath her was a beautiful pony. The lightest touch on the reins was all that was needed...

"Look out!"

Jess snapped out of her dream just in time to see her friend, Tom, wheeling a barrow full of hay directly across her path. She slammed on the brakes and her trusty steed, now a bicycle once more, swerved to the left and screeched to a halt.

"Whew. That was close," Jess gasped. She blushed wildly. "Sorry, Tom, I was miles away."

"That's OK." Tom grinned, pushing away a strand of brown hair that had fallen across his face. He continued on with his wheelbarrow, whistling softly.

Jess shook her head. Of all the people to look clumsy in front of, why did it have to be Tom? He was easily the best rider at Sandy Lane. He even had his own horse, Chancey, who was kept at half-boarding at the stables. Although Chancey was ridden by everyone, he only had eyes for Tom. Jess sighed, turning her bicycle toward the tack room.

"Hey, Jess, hang on a moment!" Her best friend, Rosie, came pedaling up the driveway, her blonde ponytail flying in the breeze. "Did you earn yourself a free ride this morning?"

"Yes. I'm going on the eleven o'clock ride. And something else happened too," Jess added. "I made friends with a new pony."

"A new pony?" Rosie was immediately interested. "Where? Whose?"

"It was a palomino mare," Jess began. "Her name's Goldie. She came running into the stable yard."

"A palomino." Rosie sighed. "How nice."

"I had to hold out my arms and stop her, Rosie," Jess said proudly. "She was charging toward me, really, really fast."

"Lucky she didn't trample you." Rosie shivered. "Why was she running into Sandy Lane anyway?"

Jess explained about the red-faced man. "The

palomino belongs to his daughter. He didn't seem to know much about ponies at all."

By now they had reached the fence beside the tack room. All the regular junior Sandy Lane riders chained their bicycles here. There was Tom's green racer, and Charlie's shiny black mountain bike too. Rosie parked her bike neatly as Jess dumped hers down on the ground.

"Come on, you two, stack those bikes neatly." Nick Brooks appeared on the steps of the tack room, blinking painfully in the bright April sunshine. "This is a stables, not a junk yard."

Jess stood her bike up swiftly.

"Ooo, I'm getting too old for dancing all night," he groaned. "My legs are killing me. Thanks for helping this morning, Jess," he added. "The list for the eleven o'clock ride is on the notice board. You're on Minstrel." He walked off, rather stiffly, across the stable yard.

Rosie followed Jess into the tack room. "Great," she said as she ran her hand down the list of riders and ponies and saw her name next to Pepper's.

"I don't know what you see in that pony." Jess wrinkled her nose. "He's so stubborn."

"Only with everyone else," Rosie reasoned. "He's always been a dream with me."

"It's because you're such a fantastic rider," Charlie teased, appearing beside them. He ran a hand through his grubby blond hair. Rosie gave an embarrassed laugh, but Jess kept quiet. Charlie was right. Rosie was a fantastic rider, even if she was too modest to admit it.

Jess didn't begrudge Rosie her riding ability, but she couldn't help feeling envious of her best friend's calmness and poise. When Rosie sat on a horse she looked completely in control.

Not like me, Jess thought.

"You're a good rider, Jess," Nick had often commented. "But it's your style that lets you down. Try and be slightly less messy when you ride."

Rosie was never messy, thought Jess. Rosie was neat – and patient too. Maybe that's why Pepper responded so well to her.

But I had patience this morning, Jess told herself. And I was calm. I couldn't have stopped that runaway pony if I hadn't been...

Her thoughts were interrupted by a light tap from Rosie's crop. "Hey! You're supposed to be using that on the ponies, not me," Jess said indignantly.

"You need some waking up today, Jess." Rosie laughed. "I've asked you five times to pass the hoof pick. Come on, it's almost time for our ride."

"Sorry. I was dreaming of that beautiful palomino."

"I wonder why we've never seen her around here before," Rosie said as they left the tack room. "Is she stabled nearby?"

"I'm not sure," Jess admitted. She reached Minstrel's stall and absent-mindedly patted the skewbald's neck. He pushed his nose down into her shoulder.

Rosie moved away toward Pepper's stall. "See you when I've tacked up," she called. "What did you do with that hoof pick by the way?"

"What? Oh, it's still in my hand, sorry." Jess handed the pick to Rosie and unbolted Minstrel's door. She tacked him up quickly and joined the rest of the ride in the stable yard. Tom was there on Chancey and Charlie waved down at Jess from Napoleon, a huge horse of 16.2 hands.

"My dad took me out to dinner at that new restaurant near Ash Hill last night," Charlie called, leaning forward in the saddle. "You know, the one where they have live bands. It was amazing."

Jess flashed Charlie a smile. He was always trying to impress, but she didn't mind. She knew things hadn't been easy for him since his parents' divorce. He didn't see much of his dad these days.

"Sounds great," she said. "Lucky you."

"Come on, you guys," a voice broke in.

It was Sarah. She was waiting to lead the trail ride. There were dark shadows under her eyes, but she was smiling. "Let's get going."

In no time at all, the ride was out of the stables and walking in single file down the lane. Sarah rode

Storm Cloud as she led them up the bumpy old coastal track toward the lighthouse. Jess could already feel Minstrel leaning on the bit.

"OK, we'll gallop across the grass. It's nice and flat," Sarah called out as they neared the lighthouse. "We'll head toward Larkfield Thicket. Stop on the edge of it and don't let the ponies run away with you. We don't want anyone scalped by the trees. Okay then, at my signal."

Then they were off, galloping across the field. Jess gave Minstrel his head and they flew across the ground. Thundering to a stop where the grass met the trees, Jess gave a whoop of joy. Nothing could match being out on a pony on a crisp day.

"Pepper's doing really well," Rosie cried as she drew alongside Jess.

"So's Minstrel," Jess replied. "Isn't this fantastic?"

At the end of the hour, the ride wound its way back to the stables. As they dismounted in the stable yard, Alex and Kate Hardy, the last of the regular junior riders, came racing up to greet them.

"Weren't you booked on the eleven o'clock?" Jess called out as she ran Minstrel's stirrups up.

"No, I've got a lunchtime lesson," Kate replied, giving Minstrel a pat. "And Alex is riding later."

"Well you missed a great ride," Rosie joined in.

"But it was a good thing I was here," Kate replied mysteriously. "There's pony trouble afoot!"

Jess laughed. Kate could be rather dramatic sometimes. "What are you talking about, Kate? It sounds exciting."

"Not really," Kate admitted. "In fact it's kind of a sad story. A girl came into the stable yard just now saying her pony's missing. She wondered if anyone had seen it. Apparently she keeps it in a field a few miles up the road and this morning when the girl – Belinda her name was – went to get her pony..."

"...it had vanished!" Alex barged in on his sister's conversation. "The pony's gate was open so it must have escaped."

"What does it look like?" Charlie joined in.

"What's its name?" Tom asked.

"Um, she says it's a palomino mare," Alex answered, "called Golddust."

Jess was immediately alert. "It sounds like the pony I saw this morning..." she cried.

"But that one was named Goldie," said Rosie.

"Goldie, Golddust, pretty similar names..." Alex pondered.

"Well, she's left her cell phone number," Kate said, handing Jess a scrap of paper.

"Belinda Lang," Jess read hesitantly. "Palomino pony. Golddust. Maybe I'll call her once I've taken care of Minstrel," she said aloud to no one in particular.

As Jess rubbed Minstrel down with absent-minded strokes she thought about Goldie and the man chasing her, and about Belinda too.

"I wonder if it could be the same pony," she reasoned aloud to Minstrel. "A man catching a pony, then this girl saying her pony's lost. I'm sure there must be an explanation for it all." She shrugged her shoulders and gave the pony a final pat. Fingering the scrap of paper in her jodhpur pocket she walked over to the tack room. But when she got there, Nick was standing at the door, surrounded by the others.

"I've got some news," Nick said to them all. "Come and sit down."

Everyone piled in and Nick smiled at the expectant faces turned toward him. He leaned against the messy desk where the rides were booked, and folded his arms.

"As you are probably aware," he began, "the Southdown Show is three weeks away."

How could they not be aware? Southdown! It was one of the most prestigious shows in the area – better even than the Benbridge Show, where Sandy Lane had done so well in the past. Last year Jess had gone to watch with the Sandy Lane regulars and had loved every minute of it.

"Well, this year at Southdown," Nick continued, ignoring the murmurs of anticipation, "there's to be a special showjumping event for juniors and I've been invited to enter three riders. It's a great honor.

I'm just sorry not all of you will be able to take part."

Nick's last words echoed in Jess's head.

Please, please choose me, she thought.

Everyone began talking at once.

"The Southdown Show – fantastic!"

"It's a real horse show."

"Even my mom's heard of it!"

"Which horses will you take?"

"Who will you enter?"

At this last question, everyone turned back to Nick. Who would he choose?

Nick shuffled the papers in front of him, biding his time. "Well, there's valuable experience to be gained from taking part in such a major event."

Jess held her breath.

"So," Nick continued. "I think that the riders who would most benefit from this sort of competition right now are Tom, Charlie..."

Tom grinned wildly, while Charlie gave a whoop and shot his fist in the air.

"Thank you," Nick continued dryly, "and Rosie."

Suddenly Jess felt as though she was looking at everyone through the wrong end of a telescope. From far away Nick's voice went on.

"Tom will ride Chancey, Charlie will be on Napoleon and Rosie will take Pepper. As I said, the show's in three weeks. Everyone should work hard in lessons until then, whether you're competing or not. I'm sorry you can't all take part, but there will be other shows and other chances. You're all excellent riders and your times will come."

Then Nick pushed his chair away from the table and stood up. "Now haven't you got jobs to do?" he said, smiling. And that was that.

"Sandy Lane at the Southdown Show," Kate cried, breaking the silence that followed Nick's departure. "Congrats, you three."

"We haven't actually done anything yet," Tom said cheerfully.

"Ah, but you will," said Alex, nudging him. "You cleaned up at the Benbridge Show last year. You can do the same at Southdown."

"You bet we can." Charlie grinned. "The question is, who'll come first?"

"I'll just be glad to get around the course," Rosie commented.

"You'll be great, Rosie," Jess managed at last. "Congratulations."

Rosie shot her friend an apologetic look. "I don't think I filled Pepper's hay net. Come with me, will you, Jess?" she asked.

"OK." Jess shrugged, following Rosie out of the tack room. The little piebald looked up, surprised to see them again so soon.

"I have no idea why Nick picked me, Jess," Rosie said softly, drawing back the bolt. "It's a complete surprise."

"Don't be silly, Rosie. You're a really good rider." Jess sighed, picking splinters of wood from Pepper's stall door.

"But you're miles more confident than me, Jess," Rosie wailed. "My legs are shaking even at the thought of it."

Jess tried to grin. "You'll be fine," she croaked at last. "Especially with me there to cheer you on. So... Bring on Southdown!"

"But not too quickly," Rosie groaned.

A little while later, Jess was wheeling her bicycle across the stable yard when Nick stopped her.

"Thanks again for getting the ponies' breakfasts this morning, Jess," he said. "And don't be too disappointed about Southdown. The thing is, it's quite a disciplined event. I'm not sure it's right for you at the moment."

"I know." Jess sighed. "I'm a clumsy rider. I've got no poise."

"Nonsense." Nick laughed. "Although I'm glad to see you're being self-critical – that's an important quality for a showjumper. You're a dedicated and instinctive rider, Jess. Your chance will come."

Instinctive, Nick had said. *Dedicated.* Suddenly everything was all right again. The gray cloud of gloom that had floated into Jess's view lifted and the sun poked through.

"Really?" Jess answered.

"Yes." Nick grinned. "Really."

When Jess returned home later that afternoon she was in a much better mood. She laid the table for supper and cleaned up without even being asked.

"What's gotten into you?" her mother asked.

"Nothing!" said Jess cheerfully.

It was only as she was undressing for bed that Jess remembered about the runaway palomino. She had completely forgotten to call Belinda.

"It's too late now." Jess groaned aloud. "I'll have to do it first thing tomorrow."

Jess crawled under her quilt. When she finally managed to sleep, she dreamed of the runaway pony jumping a clear round at Southdown. But, try as she might, Jess couldn't see who was riding her...

Chapter 3

Jumping Lesson

"The person you are calling is unavailable," a mechanical female voice intoned. "Please leave a message after the beep."

Jess grimaced. She hated leaving voice messages, so decided to send a text instead.

"Belinda," she tapped. "I think I've seen your pony. My name is Jess Adams and I'll be at Sandy Lane Stables all day." She pressed send and checked the time on her phone. Twenty minutes until the next lesson. They were practicing jumping today and all the regular junior riders were taking part.

Jess raced over to Minstrel's stall. Storm Cloud was looking over her door and whinnied as Jess went by. Jess grinned and reached into her jodhpur pocket for the sugar lump she had saved especially for her.

"Here you go, Stormy," she whispered in the pony's ear. "Don't tell anyone else, or they'll all want one."

Storm Cloud tossed her mane in conspiratorial reply and crunched on the tasty treat.

"See you later," Jess called as she went to get Minstrel ready.

Rosie was next door, tacking up Pepper. "I hope the jumps aren't too high," she said as they led the ponies out of their stalls and took them down the driveway to the outdoor arena.

"Bring your horses into the middle here," Nick called as they approached. "And I'll hold them while you walk the course."

"This sounds serious," Rosie muttered, as she followed Jess through the gate.

There were eight obstacles in all, starting with some cross poles and ending with a small wall. There was also a low but tricky double in the middle.

"They look pretty difficult," Rosie said to Jess as they walked back to get Minstrel and Pepper.

"Only because Nick has tried to set up an official course." Jess smiled. "We've jumped higher before."

"Okay," said Nick. "So what do you think?" He turned to them and smiled. "I was tempted to bring along a bell and a loud speaker – just like a real showjumping competition."

Everyone groaned.

"Don't worry," Nick continued. "These jumps are no harder than the ones you're used to. They shouldn't present many problems."

Jess turned to Rosie and smiled encouragingly.

"Piece of cake," Charlie said in Jess's ear as he rode by on Napoleon.

"OK, you guys," Nick called from the ground. "We've got work to do here. Some of you," he shot a quick glance at Charlie, "may think this course is too easy. However, there's more to a successful round than just getting over the jumps. Getting a fast time with no faults requires planning and preparation. There are no shortcuts. That's why it's essential to walk the course first. Got that?"

They all nodded vigorously.

"Good," Nick said. "Tom, would you like to test the course for us, please?"

Tom smiled ruefully and urged Chancey forward. The pair jumped swiftly with fluid movement.

"Tom makes it look so easy," Rosie breathed as he jumped the wall and rode out clear.

"He's fantastic," Jess agreed.

"Well done, Tom," said Nick. "Now, who wants to go next?"

Before anyone had a chance to answer, Charlie stormed ahead on Napoleon and jumped clear. Jess was just thinking how like a real showjumper he looked, when Nick's words cut across her.

"Not bad, Charlie," he said. "Let's have a little more thought and a little less flourish though. You almost skidded poor Napoleon on some of those turns."

Charlie reddened and Jess felt a pang of sympathy.

For the first time, she began to feel a little nervous. If Nick finds fault with Charlie, what's he going to think about my jumping? she wondered.

Rosie took the course next. She wasn't fast but she was steady, popping Pepper over the jumps in a self-contained way. Jess could see why Nick believed Rosie had a chance at Southdown.

"Your turn, Jess," Nick called, as Rosie rode out of the ring. "Take it slowly. Think of your center line and keep the jumps directly in your sight as you approach."

Jess nodded and turned Minstrel toward the first. She knew the course wasn't that difficult and tried to approach the first jump with confidence. Minstrel took it in his stride and Jess began to enjoy herself. Suddenly the double loomed sooner than she had anticipated.

"I haven't judged the pacing correctly," she muttered to herself as she felt Minstrel alter his stride. She repeated Nick's advice: "Think of your center line...keep the jumps in your sight..."

Crack! Minstrel just clipped the top pole of the second part of the double. It rocked precariously and fell to the ground with a thud. Jess's heart plummeted.

"A little impulsive, Jess," Nick said as she finished. "That's four faults. If it's any consolation, your time was fast."

Jess tried to smile, but she was annoyed with herself. If she had been more careful she would have jumped clear.

"Come on, Hector," Alex urged, as he rode him forward. Hector, practically a carthorse at over 16 hands, took the jumps slowly and steadily with a lumbering stride, but they made it.

"Good work, Alex," Nick called. "You did well to push Hector around that course. OK, Kate. It's your turn to jump."

Jess's brain was whirring. *I'm the only one to have misjudged the jumps so far...*

She was so wrapped up in herself that she wasn't even watching Kate's round on the bay pony, Jester.

"Oh!" Rosie gasped and Jess looked up to see Jester

running out at the brush.

"Do you know what you did wrong, Kate?" Nick called over to her.

"Yes," Kate answered miserably. "I checked him too early."

"Well, learn from your mistakes," said Nick. "Have another try at that one."

Kate turned Jester and introduced him again to the jump. Face set in grim determination, she gave the signal just at the right moment, and Jester flew over the brush with inches to spare.

Outside in the lane after the lesson, Jess swung herself down from Minstrel's saddle. Taking the pony by the reins she led her toward the loose stalls. Rosie came up behind them, leading Pepper and grinning wildly.

"You jumped really well, Rosie," Jess said.

"You were faster than me, though," Rosie offered in reply. "Oh that was fantastic, Jess. I don't know why I always get so nervous before a lesson. I love it when I'm there."

The two friends led the ponies into the stable yard and began rubbing them down after the sweaty ride.

Alex and Charlie were halfway through their chores as Jess and Rosie tied up Minstrel and Pepper and set to work. Tom had already taken Chancey to his stall and Kate was jumping Jester one last time.

"Hey, that was a good lesson," Charlie called. "I thought we all did really well. Alex and I were just discussing who would have won the Southdown junior trophy based on today's performance."

Jess groaned. "Don't start getting all competitive on us, Charlie."

Alex laughed. "Uh oh, Charlie, looks like you've touched a raw nerve there," he grinned. "Our Jess is a little sensitive about the Southdown Show."

This was almost more than Jess could bear. She wasn't upset about Southdown. Not really. But that still didn't give Alex the right to tease her about it. He would have to be taught a lesson. Dipping a dandy brush into the pail of water, she flicked it toward Alex. Water sprayed over Charlie too. Rosie shrieked with laughter and Jess grinned triumphantly.

"Water fight!" the boys whooped excitedly.

Soon there was water everywhere and the four were drenched. Alex leaped back to avoid another soaking and knocked over a stack of yard brushes.

"What *is* going on here?" Sarah asked, as she rounded the corner of the stables. "I hate to interrupt your fun," she added, "but someone is asking for you at the tack room, Jess."

"It must be the Southdown talent scout!" Charlie couldn't help saying.

Before Jess could douse him again, Sarah spoke. "It's a girl actually. She's about your age, Jess. Says her name's Belinda. She mentioned something about a missing palomino?"

Jess's heart skipped a beat. "Did she have a pony with her?" she asked Sarah eagerly.

"No," Sarah replied. "She's alone. Come on, you guys." Sarah turned to the others. "Let's get this mess cleaned up now."

Jess cast a glance at Rosie. "I wonder if Belinda's

found Goldie yet?" she said.

"Go and find out," Rosie urged. "I'll finish up here, don't worry."

Jess gave her friend a grateful wave and raced toward the tack room. There, waiting outside the door, stood a tall, slim girl, staring into the distance. She wore soft beige jodhpurs and a white shirt. Jess was suddenly horribly aware of her own wet, disheveled appearance. Slowly she approached the girl with none of the confidence she had mustered the morning she had caught the palomino.

"H-hello," she stammered. "I'm...I'm Jess. Are you Belinda?"

The girl turned her gaze toward Jess. "That's right," answered Belinda. "You said in your text that you'd seen Golddust."

On closer inspection, Jess saw that Belinda's face was pinched and white.

"Well, I think so. A palomino mare came racing into the stable yard yesterday morning," Jess explained. "She was about 14 hands. She had the most beautiful white gold mane and flowing tail."

"That sounds like Golddust," Belinda said quickly. "I went to her field at seven yesterday morning, like I always do, and she wasn't there. So is she here now?" Belinda asked. "Did you catch her?"

"Yes, I caught her," Jess began slowly. "But she isn't here. There was a man chasing her."

"A man? What man?" Belinda suddenly looked panic-stricken.

"Um," Jess stammered. "He said Golddust...or rather Goldie...was his daughter's pony...that the pony was a devil to catch..." Jess's words came out in staccato breaths.

Belinda's face looked in blank amazement. "That's impossible," she said. "My father's dead. Golddust hasn't run away at all," she wailed, and in that moment Jess realized the awful truth. "She's been stolen!"

Chapter 4

Jess Is Sorry

Jess sat at the desk in the tack room, her head in her hands. "And I actually helped that man to steal Golddust!" she moaned. "Oh, Belinda, I'm so sorry. I'm such an idiot."

Belinda shrugged sadly. "There was no way you could have known," she began.

"How can you be so nice?" said Jess. "I'd be furious, if I were you."

Belinda sighed. "What's the point?" she reasoned. "Golddust is gone now."

At that moment, Sarah and Rosie appeared.

"Everything OK?" asked Sarah.

"Far from it!" moaned Jess. She quickly explained what had happened.

"Oh, Jess," gasped Rosie in dismay. "That man must have been a thief! But how did he know the pony's name?"

"I suppose Goldie is an obvious name for a golden palomino," said Belinda.

"We should go to the police about all this," said Sarah. Her voice was reassuring and capable. "You must give a statement, Jess. And a description of the man you saw. It might help them to find Belinda's pony sooner."

The police! Jess swallowed hard.

"I can take you now in the Land Rover, if you like," Sarah went on. "Give you some moral support."

Jess nodded gratefully. "Yes please," she replied.

"What about you, Belinda?" Sarah said gently. "Would you like to come with us?"

Belinda shook her head. "They already know Golddust is missing," she explained. "Mom took me to the police station earlier today. There's no point in me going back there again."

"Well, if you'd rather stay here and wait for us, I understand," said Sarah.

Jess didn't understand at all. If Golddust was her pony she'd be wanting to check the police station every five minutes for news.

"I'll stay with you if you like, Belinda," Rosie said, looking hesitantly at her. "There's some lemonade in the fridge. Would you like some?"

Belinda shrugged her shoulders. "All right."

Jess shot Rosie a look of thanks and followed Sarah to the Land Rover.

At the police station, Jess had to go over the whole morning in tiny detail. "You will find Golddust won't you?" she asked, concerned. "And catch the thief."

"We'll do our best," the friendly desk sergeant assured her.

"What do you think he might have done with Golddust?" Jess asked.

The sergeant shrugged. "Well, he could be

planning to sell her at auction. He could have a private buyer..."

Jess sat hunched miserably in the Land Rover on the short drive back to Sandy Lane.

"These things happen, Jess," Sarah said to her. "It's why we have to be extra-cautious about security. I'm afraid ponies are easy targets."

Rosie was waiting eagerly for Jess in the tack room, but there was no sign of Belinda.

"How did it go?" Rosie asked.

"Oh, all right I suppose," Jess replied, sinking down into the old basket chair in the corner of the room. "The police aren't exactly rushing around with sniffer dogs and magnifying glasses though."

Rosie laughed. "Well I guess they know what they're doing," she said.

"Where's Belinda?" Jess asked.

"She's gone home," Rosie replied.

"Gone home?" Jess was incredulous. "Why? If my pony was missing I'd be out there looking, not sitting at home. Honestly, she hardly seemed angry or upset. I feel really worried and nervous for Golddust and she isn't even my pony!"

"Belinda's upset." Rosie paused as she tried to explain. "She's just not showing it the way you would. Listen – she told me her dad died six months ago and she's just moved to Asheville where she doesn't know anybody and now her pony's been stolen. If that had happened to me I'd probably lock myself in my bedroom and bawl my head off for months."

Jess was silent for a moment. She hadn't thought of it like that. Then she perked up. "So it's a good thing she's met us," she cried.

"Why's that?" Rosie said slowly.

"We're going to find Golddust for her."

"We?" Rosie croaked.

"Yes! It's the least I can do," Jess continued. "Belinda won't be miserable for long. Not with Jess Adams and Rosie Edwards on Golddust's trail!"

Chapter 5

Near Disaster

The next day was Monday and Jess was at the stables again. She was hoping to ask Nick about upcoming horse sales, in case the thief tried to sell Golddust quickly.

"Hello, Stormy," she said, passing the beautiful gray's stall. "You're looking lovely today."

"Jess," Nick called, walking across the stable yard. "I've got a job for you. Sarah's at the saddler's and I have to go to the feed store. Could you tack up Minstrel for a ride in twenty minutes?"

"Yes, of course," said Jess. "Who's riding?"

"A new girl, name Marissa Slater. Tom's taking her out. I know her father vaguely. He seems to think Marissa's quite a good rider, says he's going to buy her a pony of her own soon."

"Lucky her." Jess sighed.

Nick laughed sympathetically. "Well, he wants Marissa to try out Sandy Lane first and if she likes it, I hope she'll come back. We need the business," he muttered, almost to himself.

Before Jess could ask about horse sales, Nick had climbed into his Land Rover and driven off.

Jess went to get Minstrel's saddle from its hook and realized that Chancey's tack was still in its place. It wasn't like Tom to be late. Then the tack room door swung open and Tom stumbled inside.

"There you are," Jess said. "I was beginning to worry. You've got a ride in ten minutes. Someone named Marissa Slater. What a name!"

Jess stopped abruptly as she saw Tom's face. It was ghostly white.

"Are you all right?" she asked. "You look awful."

"I'm not sure." Tom collapsed heavily into the wicker chair. "I feel terrible. I've just cycled here and my stomach's killing me. I feel all hot and shaky."

"Oh poor you," Jess sympathized. "Maybe you ate something bad?"

"Ow ow ow," Tom groaned. "No, it feels worse than that. I don't think I can take that ride, Jess. I can hardly stand straight. Where's Nick?"

"He's gone to get some feed. And Sarah's at the saddler's. What are we going to do, Tom? I could try Nick's cell phone but she'll be here any minute."

"Well, we'll just have to ask her to come back another day," Tom said.

"Or I could take her out!" Jess cried impulsively. "Turning her away would be bad for business. That's what Nick would say."

Tom managed a half smile, despite his obvious pain. "Well," he began. "Nick has let you take a ride before, hasn't he?"

"Yes, I've done it twice," Jess replied proudly.

Tom made up his mind quickly. "Go on then,"

he said. "You've got two ponies to tack up in under ten minutes!"

"OK." Jess smiled happily. She wanted a chance to prove she was responsible and capable. Everyone had heard the story of Golddust by now, how she had practically given the pony to a thief. She was determined to show everyone, especially Tom and Nick, that she wasn't a complete idiot. "I'd better ride Hector," she called to Tom. "He's reliable."

But Tom was silent, his face pinched with pain.

Jess raced to the stalls. She had just finished Minstrel and was on her way back for Hector's tack when a shiny white Range Rover pulled into the yard. A haughty looking girl about Jess's age stepped out, wearing immaculate fawn jodhpurs and holding a black riding crop. A tall man got out from the driver's side and turned a questioning gaze on Jess.

"I booked a ride for my daughter," he began.

"They do know that, Dad," the girl hissed loudly.

"Ah yes," the man agreed.

What a snooty girl, Jess thought. Aloud she said,

"Are you Marissa Slater?"

"Yes I am," the girl replied, primly.

"All right. Well, hello," Jess continued. "I'm Jess Adams, and I'll be taking you out today. And this," she said turning to Minstrel, "is the pony you'll be riding, Minstrel."

Marissa looked scornfully at the pony.

"Bit of a nag, isn't she? She doesn't look very fast."

"She's a he, actually." Jess flushed angrily. Did this girl really know anything about riding? How dare she call Minstrel a nag? "He loves galloping," she said, trying to sound friendly.

Marissa wasn't impressed. "No, he won't do at all," she said, waving her riding crop dismissively. "Ah, now that's the kind of thing I should be riding."

Jess turned to where Marissa was pointing – right at Storm Cloud, who was hanging her head over her stall door as usual.

"Oh I'm sorry," Jess said quickly. "That's Storm Cloud. No one's allowed to take her out unless they've been riding here for a while. She's part-Arab and really precious. She's also on the flighty side and a bit unpredictable."

"Exactly what I'm looking for," said Marissa. "I am an experienced rider, you know." She turned to the man with her. "Daddy, tell the girl I can ride who I like."

"Well," Mr. Slater began. "That horse…"

"Pony," Jess muttered.

"Um, pony. She does look nice. So what's the problem?" he asked. "Where's Nick Brooks?"

"He had to go out." Jess shifted uncomfortably. She could feel the situation slipping away from her.

"Daddy, if you're going to make me ride at this stables before I'm allowed my own pony at least let me ride who I want," Marissa interrupted peevishly.

"All right my pet," Mr. Slater soothed, and Jess began to feel sick.

"Here's how it is," he said, addressing himself firmly to Jess. "Marissa will ride that Storm Cloud creature now and I'll square it with Nick later. We're old friends, you know, and I am paying for this."

Jess was furious, but managed to bite her tongue. Well, if Marissa and her dad wouldn't listen to her advice, that was their problem. Handing Minstrel's reins to Marissa, she ran to the tack room to get Storm Cloud's things. Deep down, Jess knew it was a bad idea, but Mr. Slater had been so insistent, she couldn't back out now.

She tacked up Storm Cloud and led her out of her stall. The little pony was excited and Marissa could barely mount her as she skipped and pirouetted around the stable yard.

"See you later, Daddy," Marissa called and then she was off down the lane at a brisk walk. Jess winced as Marissa sawed furiously on the reins and waved her crop dangerously high around the pony's eyes. Jess urged Minstrel into a lively trot and followed them out of the stable yard.

"She's raring to go," Marissa called over her shoulder.

Jess nudged Minstrel on and overtook Marissa. She led them along the bumpy coastal track and on toward the lighthouse.

"There are some good places to gallop around here," she called back to Marissa.

To the right of them the grass stretched away invitingly, and Jess could feel that Minstrel was eager for a race. Storm Cloud was positively foaming at the mouth. The more the pony pulled, the tighter Marissa tugged at the reins, until poor Stormy's ears were almost touching the girl's turned-up nose.

"Maybe you should give her a little more rein," said Jess. "And stop waving that crop. Then she'd calm down a little."

"Nonsense," Marissa sneered. "You have to show them who's boss. Besides, who wants to ride a calm pony? This is far more exciting. I'm off!"

She gave Storm Cloud a terrific whack with the crop and for a fraction of a second Storm Cloud seemed to hover in mid-air, almost stunned by the pain. Then she shot off and bolted across the field.

Marissa pulled desperately on the reins, but it was too late. She had lost control.

"You stupid girl," Jess cried in dismay and disbelief. She watched helplessly as the fragile gray careened across the fields at breakneck speed. Storm Cloud was headed straight for Larkfield Thicket and Marissa couldn't turn her.

The thought of the low-hanging branches spurred Jess into action. She urged Minstrel into a gallop and he raced off, mane and tail flying in the breeze.

Ahead, Marissa screamed loudly and shut her eyes tight with terror. Minstrel's pounding hooves rang in Jess's ears and her eyes streamed with water as the wind bit into her face. Faster and faster Minstrel raced. Storm Cloud was well in front, but she was weaving from side to side. Jess concentrated on keeping Minstrel on a straight line, and soon they were gaining on them. All the time the low-hanging branches of Larkfield Thicket loomed nearer.

At last they were galloping alongside Storm Cloud, only feet away from the trees. Marissa had dropped Storm Cloud's reins and was clinging to his mane. With a supreme effort, Jess leaned over as far as she dared and grabbed Storm Cloud's reins. It seemed the only thing to do. She pulled hard and brought Storm Cloud's head around to the left, turning Minstrel at just the same time.

Storm Cloud seemed surprised that someone had taken charge and followed immediately. But Marissa didn't change direction and went flying forward, sailing over Storm Cloud's neck. She landed with a thump in a patch of mud at the edge of the trees.

Jess brought Minstrel to a stop alongside the field and Storm Cloud followed. As she gathered up Storm Cloud's reins, the little gray sprang back nervously. Her nostrils quivered and her heaving flanks were covered in foam and sweat.

"Whoa there, Stormy," Jess cooed softly, jumping to the ground. "You're all right now."

Slowly, Storm Cloud calmed down. She listened intently to Jess and nuzzled her nose wearily into Jess's shoulder.

"Are you all right?" Jess called over to Marissa.

"No, of course I'm not all right," the girl howled. "That wretched animal is dangerous. She shouldn't be allowed out."

Jess was furious. "You insisted on riding her. Couldn't you see that she was worked up already? The last thing she needed was a beating from a crop to get her going."

"How...how dare you!" Marissa retorted. "You're the one to blame. You and this stupid horse. I wasn't properly supervised. Just wait, I'm going to report you to—"

"What's going on?" a familiar voice interrupted.

Jess spun around. Nick was striding toward them, his Land Rover parked hastily in the field. Jess's relief soon gave way to trepidation.

"I was worried when I saw that Storm Cloud was missing," said Nick sternly. "What's happened? Where's Tom?"

Quickly Jess explained everything – Tom's illness, Marissa's insistence on riding Storm Cloud and Jess's own eagerness to help.

Nick took a deep breath. "Well, we'll talk about this later, Jess," he said. "Are you OK?" he asked, turning to Marissa. "Can you stand up?"

Marissa got shakily to her feet. She swayed a little and Nick held out a steadying hand. "Take it slowly now," he said.

"I'm all right," Marissa said fiercely. Her face was determined, but Jess saw tears in her eyes.

"I'll take you back in the Land Rover," Nick said gently. "Jess can lead Minstrel and Storm Cloud."

"No!" Marissa cried. Then, seeing Nick's surprise she tried to explain. "I mean...I can't let my father see me like this. You won't tell him, will you?" She looked at Nick pleadingly.

"Well, I don't know..." Nick began.

"If he hears about this he'll never let me have my own pony," she continued. "Not a really good one, anyway. He'll get me some safe, plodding old thing."

Nick shook his head slowly. "You can't fool him that you're a better rider than you are, Marissa," he said. "Look, why don't you take a few lessons at

Sandy Lane first? I think you'd find it a big help. Even the best riders still have lessons," he added before Marissa could protest. "And the more experience you have, the more you'll enjoy having your own pony."

"Well..." Marissa hesitated. "If I come and ride at Sandy Lane, will you promise not to tell my father what's happened today?"

Jess let out a gasp. Imagine talking to Nick like that! Even Nick seemed a little taken aback. When he finally replied, his voice was serious.

"I don't make bargains, Marissa," he said. "And I do think you need some more practice. Now, do you think you can ride Minstrel back, under Jess's supervision?" Marissa nodded quickly.

"OK. Good girl," said Nick. He turned to Jess. "You ride Storm Cloud back, Jess – and I'd like a word with you once you've untacked the ponies."

Then he strode back to the Land Rover.

It was a moment before Jess came to her senses. Nick had told her to ride Storm Cloud. Not in the arena, not around the stable yard, but out in the open – and after Storm Cloud had bolted too. For a moment, she wasn't even bothered about what Nick would say back at the stables. Right now all that mattered was Storm Cloud.

She gathered up the reins and mounted. "Walk," she said softly, and Storm Cloud moved forward.

Jess glanced back. Marissa was following on Minstrel. She was calmer now, and Jess noted that she really wasn't such a bad rider when she wasn't showing off.

Storm Cloud's step was quick and eager as Jess kept a light but steadying control on the rein. Jess longed to gallop – she knew Storm Cloud would go like the wind – but she stopped herself.

"Not this time, Stormy," she murmured. "We'd better go home."

Chapter 6

A Turn of Events

"What exactly was wrong with Tom then?" Nick asked, in a stern voice.

"He said he felt sick," Jess answered quietly. "So I offered to take Marissa out."

Jess stood in Nick and Sarah's kitchen, staring at the cracked red linoleum floor. Nick was leaning against the sink, his arms folded.

"I've given you permission to take rides before Jess, but Tom's much more experienced than you."

Jess swallowed hard, trying to hold back her tears.

"And I think you know that Storm Cloud was the

wrong choice for Marissa," Nick went on.

Jess nodded miserably. "I'm sorry, Nick. I did try to warn Marissa, but Mr. Slater said he knew you and that it would be all right."

"I don't know him that well," Nick continued. "But I do appreciate it's difficult to go against an adult's wishes."

"I'm sorry," Jess croaked again.

"Anyway, I was impressed with the way you handled Storm Cloud. You remained calm and thoughtful in a potentially dangerous situation. Nice job."

Jess blushed furiously.

"All right. Lecture over." Nick gestured with a nod toward the door. "Go back to the stable yard. It must be lunchtime."

Jess gave a grateful wave and hurried to the tack room. There was no one there so she settled down by herself to eat her sandwiches. As she munched, she flicked through the local paper and her eyes were drawn to a list of open air markets.

"Benbridge Women's Institute Floral Display..." she read. "Livestock day at Bucknell Pig Farm..."

She ran her finger down the small black lettering, until she found what she was looking for: "The Ash Hill Horse Sale. 2nd Thursday of every month. Horses and ponies for sale at auction. 10 a.m. at Ash Hill Showground."

Jess did some rapid calculating. It was Monday the 8th today – the second Monday of the month – so the sale was in three days.

"Caught you!" A voice shouted in her ear. Jess jumped up and the paper slid to the floor.

"Hard at work, looking for Golddust already I see." Rosie grinned.

"Yes, it's time I got something right." Jess sighed.

"What's happened this time?" Rosie grinned. "Don't tell me. More runaway ponies? International horse thieves?"

Jess laughed and told Rosie all about the ride with Marissa.

"Marissa Slater?" Rosie wrinkled up her nose.

"I've not heard of her. She doesn't go to our school."

"Thank goodness," Jess said. "Anyway, we've got more important things to think about." She picked up the paper and stabbed at it with her forefinger. "There's a sale at Ash Hill in three days. It only happens once a month so the man who stole Golddust can't have been yet."

"That's where Nick bought Storm Cloud..."

"Well that's a good omen." Jess smiled cheerfully.

Just then, Alex and Kate came bounding in, arguing as usual. Charlie followed close behind and greeted everyone with a casual wave.

"Has anyone seen Tom?" Jess asked.

They all shook their heads.

"But he should be here soon for the jumping lesson," Alex said.

"I'm sorry, I'm afraid he won't be." Sarah appeared on the step of the tack room. "I've got some bad news," she said solemnly. "Tom's mother called to say he's been taken to the hospital."

"Hospital?" Alex gasped. "What's wrong?"

"They're not sure at the moment," Sarah replied. "He has severe stomach pains. You saw him this morning, didn't you, Jess?"

Jess nodded. "He looked awful."

"Well he's in the best place now," Sarah assured them. "He insisted his mother call us to say he couldn't make his lesson. He wanted to make sure Chancey's not left out."

"Typical Tom." Alex tried to laugh, but Jess could see he was worried. The others just looked dumbstruck.

"As soon as I have any more news I'll let you know," said Sarah briskly. "Now haven't you all got a jumping lesson? Don't keep Nick waiting. I'll exercise Chancey."

"Yes, come on everyone," said Charlie, gruffly. "Worrying isn't going to win us any trophies."

"I wish we knew what was wrong with Tom," Alex groaned as the lesson came to an end. It had been a subdued hour. They had all jumped well, but without enthusiasm. Jess had cleared the course, but unspectacularly, all her thoughts on Tom.

"Tom's mother is bound to call again when there's any more news," said Rosie when they had finished with the ponies. "Let's hang around in case there's a phone call."

"OK," Jess agreed.

They flopped down on some hay bales behind the big barn. To take their minds off Tom, Jess told Rosie her plans for finding Golddust. "Apart from going to Ash Hill, I thought we should put posters up – at farriers' and vets', local events, that kind of thing, as well as asking at other riding stables..."

Rosie stopped Jess with a laugh. "Aren't you forgetting something?"

"What?" Jess asked eagerly.

"Belinda!" Rosie said. "Shouldn't she be involved in this? After all, Golddust is her pony."

"Oh yes." Jess paused. "Maybe Belinda would feel happier if she put her mind on finding Golddust."

"And if she knew we wanted to help she might feel better too," Rosie pointed out.

"You're right, Rosie," Jess said. "I'll call her now."

"Take it slowly, Jess," said Rosie. "You don't want to frighten her off. You can be a little bit, well, overwhelming sometimes."

"I know." Jess smiled.

Just then, Kate came racing toward them. "Come quickly!" she called. "Sarah's got news about Tom."

Jess and Rosie raced after Kate to join Charlie and Alex in the tack room.

"It's appendicitis," Sarah announced. "Tom's going to have an operation this afternoon. He'll be in the hospital for several days. But it will be a while before he's completely better."

"When will he be able to ride again?" Alex asked.

"A month or so," said Sarah, "maybe more."

"So he'll miss Southdown?" Charlie said.

"It looks like it," Sarah replied.

"Poor Tom," said Rosie.

"Poor Chancey," said Jess.

Jess was still thinking about Tom that evening as she cycled through Asheville and on to the new houses at the edge of town, where Belinda lived.

Belinda had been hesitant on the phone, but Jess sensed a hint of curiosity in her voice. In her mind, Jess had already found Golddust and was receiving Belinda's heart-felt thanks. Lost in thought, Jess cycled straight past Belinda's house.

"Missed it." She turned her bike sharply and pedaled back until she spotted number 3412. This was it. A small stone statue of a dancing horse stood guard on the front step.

"You must be Jess," Belinda's mother said as she opened the door. "Come in." She called up the stairs. "Belinda...you have a visitor!"

Belinda appeared on the landing. She was wearing jeans and a dark blue hoodie, her hair pulled back in a ponytail. "Hi, Jess," she said, with a half smile. "I guess the police didn't have any news?" she said.

"No, sorry." Jess shook her head.

Belinda shrugged. "Oh... You can come up to my room, if you like." She disappeared through a door at the top of the stairs.

Belinda's mother smiled at them as Jess followed Belinda to her bedroom a little doubtfully.

When Jess stepped into the room, she relaxed immediately. Posters and pictures of horses and ponies stared down at Jess and there were ribbons of all colors – but mainly red, Jess noticed enviously.

"I won those with Golddust," said Belinda, following Jess's gaze. "She's a good showjumper."

"Lucky you," Jess said.

"Do you ride at Sandy Lane regularly then?" Belinda said.

"Yes," Jess replied eagerly. "I don't have my own pony or anything, but the Sandy Lane ponies are great. Especially Storm Cloud. She's my favorite."

"Is that the little gray one?" Belinda asked.

"Yes," Jess said in surprise. "How did you know?"

Belinda smiled again. "Just a guess. I noticed her when I came to the stables yesterday..." She stopped suddenly and looked sad again.

"Belinda," Jess said quickly. "Rosie and I want to help you look for Golddust. We thought we could put up posters and look around horse sales. There's one on Thursday..." She stopped and thought for a moment. "If you want our help, that is."

Belinda was quiet but her eyes were shining. "Would you really help me?" she cried at last. "Thank you!" And then she began to pour her heart out.

Jess heard how Belinda's mother had needed to find a job after Belinda's father died, how they'd had to move to Asheville and how Belinda was going to be starting at a new school after Easter. Belinda had been keeping Golddust in a field on the edge of town until her mother earned enough to pay for stabling.

Finally Belinda told Jess how seeing all the riders at Sandy Lane Stables had made her feel so lonely.

"But you're not alone now," Jess cried. "You've got Rosie and me! And we've got this horse sale to go to on Thursday."

"You're right," Belinda agreed happily. "Oh wouldn't it be wonderful if we found Golddust?"

"Yes, it would." Jess smiled and looked around at Belinda's wonderfully horsey room. "Is that you?"

she asked, pointing to a color snapshot of a girl and a pony. "Can I have a look?"

"Of course." Belinda took the photo down and gave it a quick dust with her sleeve. "It's me and Golddust at Benbridge last summer."

"The Benbridge Show?" Jess exclaimed. "How fantastic. Tom jumped there last year too. He won the open jumping." She looked down at the photo in her hands. Then she looked again.

"Hang on a minute," Jess said, her voice tightening.

"What's the matter?" said Belinda.

"This...this isn't Golddust!" she mumbled.

"Of course it's Golddust." Belinda laughed. "I should know. She is my pony."

"No, I don't mean that, I mean..." Jess swallowed hard and then the words came spilling out. "This isn't the same pony I saw at Sandy Lane the other morning. This isn't the pony I helped to catch!"

Chapter 7

Ash Hill Horse Sale

"It was awful, Rosie," Jess told her friend as they walked down the street. It was Thursday morning, the day of the Ash Hill sale, and the pair were on their way to the bus stop to meet Belinda.

Jess hadn't been able to go to Sandy Lane for a few days. She'd been kept busy by her mother and had been anxious to help out, since today she wanted to go to the horse sale, then visit Tom at the hospital. It was Nick who'd told Jess that Tom wanted to see her. He wouldn't say why, just that it was important.

Now Jess was filling Rosie in about what had

happened at Belinda's house.

"The palomino in the photo definitely wasn't the one I'd helped to catch," she explained. "The pony I saw was pure gold, but Belinda's Golddust has a circle of white hair on her forehead."

"So what did Belinda say?" Rosie was curious.

"She asked me if I was sure and then she just sat there very quietly. Which made me feel pretty miserable. I thought we'd be able to help, but now we have no idea if Golddust has been stolen, has run away, or is lying dead in a ditch somewhere."

"Well at least you know it's not your fault Golddust has disappeared, but what a mystery," said Rosie. "I wonder what happened to the palomino pony you saw then. And where it came from."

"I wish I knew," Jess replied. "I cycled to the police station and I told them that I'd made a mistake, that I hadn't seen Belinda's pony after all."

"What did they say?"

"I saw a different policeman this time. He didn't say much, but he raised his eyebrows a lot and shook his head and wrote everything down in a big book and asked me to sign my name. Oh, Rosie, is all this pointless? Going to Ash Hill, I mean...trying to help Belinda find Golddust."

"We said we'd help her look, so we must," Rosie reasoned. "Watch out, here's Belinda now," she added, seeing the tall girl at the bus stop.

"Hello," Belinda said quietly.

"Hi," said Rosie. "Jess has just been telling me about Goldie not being Golddust. It's very strange."

"Isn't it?" Belinda said as the bus appeared and they climbed aboard. "Strange that two palominos should be running loose on the same day."

Rosie didn't know what to say. They rode in silence for the rest of the way. Jess reached up to ring the bell and the bus shuddered to a stop. The doors swished open and the three girls jumped off. They followed a steady stream of cars and trailers until they came to a turn in the road and a sign in a field that said Ash Hill Horse Sale.

Weaving their way through the crowd they

eventually came to the group of horses and ponies up for auction.

"Okay, let's be logical about this," said Rosie as she bought a sale catalog. "Are there any ponies that match Golddust's description?"

Jess thumbed through the auction catalog. "If Golddust is here, she'll be a late entrant," she reasoned. "After all, there hasn't been much time between her going missing and this sale."

"That's true," Rosie agreed. "The late additions are on this slip of paper at the back. Look."

There were a few that sounded promising.

"Lot forty-two," Jess read out. "Palomino pony. 13.2 hands without shoes. Fully warranted. Hmm. A little small, but worth a look."

Belinda peered over her shoulder. "Here's another one. Lot fifty-five. Palomino show pony. 14.2 hands. Rising five. Some blemishes, but sound."

"They don't make that one sound very attractive," commented Jess. "Still, we can't afford to miss it. It's about the right height."

She turned the page. "Lot sixty-six. Registered palomino. Showjumper. 14 hands without shoes. Ideal jumper."

"That one's a possibility," Rosie chipped in. "Any more?"

Jess thumbed through the rest of the catalog and shook her head. "No, that's it."

"Good," said Rosie. "That means we can check them out quickly."

"How should we do it?" Belinda asked. "Should we wait for their numbers to be called?"

"Maybe we should have a look at them now," Rosie suggested. "Pretend we're interested buyers."

"What, three girls with only a bus fare between us?" Jess was suddenly hesitant. Then she saw Belinda's face, and she knew they had to try.

"It's the best we can do," Rosie said firmly. "Should we go together or split up?"

"Together, definitely," Belinda said.

Faced with row upon row of sad and neglected horses, Jess felt less and less cheerful. There *were* good ponies of course – the ones destined for riding stables or a lucky handful of children who would be getting their very own pony. Jess looked longingly at these fit and healthy animals. Then she thought of the runaway palomino. Where was Goldie now?

"Lot forty-two," said Rosie. "Here it is."

They drew to a halt beside a pony tethered to a pole. Belinda gave one look at the little pony and shook her head.

"Nope. This isn't her."

"That's not even a palomino!" said Jess when they came to lot fifty-five. "It's a dun. Definitely a dun."

Lot sixty-six was beautiful. A really gentle palomino with kind eyes. "But it's not Golddust." Belinda sighed, looking defeated. Jess sighed too.

"Come on," Rosie said. "I've packed a lunch. Let's share it."

Slowly they walked away from the ponies and flopped down under a tree.

"Cheese or ham sandwich?" asked Rosie.

"Cheese, please," said Jess. "Actually, I'd better get

a move on," she cried, glancing at her watch. "I'm supposed to be visiting Tom this afternoon..."

Jess caught the bus to the hospital and arrived just before visiting time. It took her several minutes to find Tom's floor.

"You look a little green," she couldn't help saying.

"Thanks a lot, Jess. You would too if someone had sliced you open, rummaged about with your insides and then stitched you back up again with a needle."

"Yuck." Jess wrinkled up her nose. She fished around in her plastic bag and pulled out a pile of dog-eared magazines. "I know people are supposed to bring flowers but I couldn't find any, so I brought you some pony magazines instead. There's a really good story in one of them about a ghost rider and a lost foal..."

Jess hovered by Tom's hospital bed, aware that she was blabbering.

There were eight rooms on Tom's wing, four of them occupied. On the other side of the hallway, a girl of about Jess's age slept soundly. Her hair was blonde and there were dark circles under her eyes.

"That's Mary," Tom said, following Jess's eye across the hallway. "She's got a pony."

"Lucky her," Jess said, as she sat down on Tom's bed. "Nick said you wanted to see me," she blurted out, curiosity getting the better of her.

Tom smiled. "So you're not just here to wish me a speedy recovery then?" he teased.

Jess looked downcast. "No. I mean..." She stopped and laughed. "Sorry, Tom. Of course I want you to get well quickly..."

"Don't worry," Tom interrupted. "I wanted to see you because we've got a proposition for you. Me and Nick, that is. Nick said I should be the one to tell you. It's about Southdown," Tom explained. "I won't be able to ride, so would you like to take my place?"

There was silence. Jess knew it was her turn to speak, but she didn't know what to say. She was going to ride at Southdown!

"I'm no replacement for you, Tom," she managed at last. "You're a much better rider than me."

"Well obviously no one expects you to do as wonderfully as I would have." Tom grinned. "Oh no, I sounded just like Charlie then, didn't I?"

"Just like him," Jess agreed happily.

"But I think you'll be in with a chance," Tom continued seriously. "I'll be out of here by then, so I can come and cheer you on."

"Oh, that would be wonderful!" Jess cried.

"How's Chancey coping without me?" asked Tom. "Is he pining away?"

"He's fine. But he does look a little sad," Jess said, trying to drag her mind back to normal conversation as little bubbles of excitement burst in her stomach. "Don't worry," she continued. "We've explained where you are and that you'll be back soon. He understands."

"Of course he does," Tom agreed. "He's a very intelligent horse. Oh look, here's my mom."

Jess turned around to see Tom's mother standing in the doorway, tall and elegant. Jess stood up to greet her. She had only met Mrs. Buchanan a few times and she wanted to make a good impression.

But as Mrs. Buchanan came nearer, the smile froze on Jess's face. Walking a few paces behind her, jacket bundled under his arm, was a stocky man. A man whose face Jess remembered well.

"You!" Jess croaked, as the man drew nearer. "You're the man with the runaway pony!"

Chapter 8

Explanations

Jess stood and stared. She knew she was being rude but she just couldn't help it. The last time she had seen this man, he had been chasing a palomino pony into the stable yard at Sandy Lane Stables.

"What's the matter, Jess?" Tom began.

Mrs. Buchanan looked shocked at her behavior, but Jess couldn't move. She was face to face with... a pony thief! She didn't know what to do. He peered at her now and a smile spread slowly across his face.

"I recognize you!" he exclaimed at last. "You're

the young lady who helped me catch Goldie the other morning!" He waved to the girl across the hallway from Tom, who was just waking up. "Mary, this is the girl I told you about – the one who stopped Goldie from running away."

Mary rubbed her eyes, propped herself up on her pillows and smiled at Jess.

"So G-Goldie is your pony," Jess stammered.

"Yes," Mary said. "I really miss her."

"You were a life saver," the man said to Jess. "I can't thank you enough. I was upset that morning because Mary had been rushed to the hospital. I was taking Goldie to be looked after by some friends and I was doing a bad job of getting her into the horse trailer. That's why she got nervous and bolted. If you hadn't caught her, I don't know what would have happened."

"She's a beautiful pony," Jess managed. She wanted to say more, but she was still in shock.

"What's your name?" the man asked.

"Jess. Jess Adams."

"I'm Bob Hughes," he replied. "Mary's father."

"Thank you so much, Jess." Mary smiled, but Jess just looked dazed.

"Would you like some water, Jess? You're looking a little unwell." Tom's mother was full of concern.

"No, I..." Jess started.

Tom began to laugh, then clutched his stomach. "Ouch, my stitches!" he yelped. "Isn't that the pony we thought had been stolen? The one that Belinda girl came looking for?" he continued.

"Stolen?" Mary's father looked astonished.

Of course, Tom didn't know that Goldie wasn't the same pony as Golddust. Jess shook her head and began to explain about Belinda's missing pony, then about mistaking Goldie for Golddust and, even worse, about reporting the incident at Sandy Lane Stables to the police.

Fortunately, Mary's dad just laughed. "So I'm a wanted man now, am I?"

But Mary looked concerned. "Poor Belinda," she said. "She must be heartbroken."

Jess nodded in silent agreement. One mystery had been solved but that still left Golddust...

Jess wished she could do more to track Golddust down, but now she had a competition to prepare for, starting with a special lesson the Saturday before Easter.

"Concentrate!" Nick called. "Come on, Jess, you're letting Minstrel get away with murder. He'll run out if you don't check him."

"Sorry, Nick," Jess mumbled. She shortened Minstrel's reins and turned again toward the first jump. This time, the little pony met the fence at exactly the right spot and they flew over the cross poles with inches to spare.

"Better," said Nick. "Much better."

With Southdown less than two weeks away, the excitement and pressure were mounting for the Sandy Lane entrants.

"We've got the evenings as well," Nick reassured them. "Don't worry, you're all doing fine."

"Tom gets out of the hospital today," Rosie said as they rode back after the lesson. "I heard Nick talking to his mom."

"I wonder how Mary is," Jess said. She had told Rosie – and Belinda – all about Mary and Goldie.

"She must miss Goldie terribly," Rosie said.

"But not as much as Belinda misses Golddust," said Jess.

Both girls were quiet for a moment. They hadn't found Golddust at Ash Hill and there weren't any more horse sales for a while. Belinda had put posters up all around the area, but there had been no response. It seemed like the end of the trail.

Frustrated she couldn't do more, Jess had asked Belinda to come to Southdown. She thought it might cheer her up.

"I'm not sure..." Belinda had replied. "I had been hoping to ride Golddust at Southdown. I'd feel awful going there without her."

Jess replayed this conversation in her head now as she led Minstrel into the stable yard.

"I'll take Minstrel," called Nick, interrupting Jess's thoughts. "He's got a lesson in a minute."

"OK," she said in surprise. "But I thought I was booked on him for a ride?"

"Sorry about that," Nick said. "You'll have to ride someone else. Let's see." He paused for a moment, mentally checking off the list of Sandy Lane ponies. "It'll have to be Storm Cloud," he said finally.

"Storm Cloud?" Jess breathed. "Really?"

"Lucky you," Rosie whispered.

"She's the only one available." Nick smiled. "Anyway, it's the least I can do, seeing as I'm commandeering Minstrel for a lesson with our old friend, Marissa. Well don't just stand there. Get Stormy tacked up."

"I'm going," Jess said quickly, before Nick could change his mind.

Fifteen minutes later, the eleven o'clock ride was ready to leave. As Sarah led the ride on Feather, Jess looked back at the stable yard to see Nick checking his watch and muttering angrily. It looked as if

Marissa was late.

"Move out, everybody," Sarah called and the ride clattered out of the stable yard and down the lane.

For the next hour, riding Storm Cloud made Jess forget Marissa; forget mistaking Bob Hughes for a thief; forget Golddust even. It was such a treat to be riding the little gray, with her light and easy step and her ears pricked forward, alert and attentive.

They reached the open fields at the back of the stables and Sarah gathered the ride around her.

"Those who want to can gallop to the end of the field. There are three cross-country fences to jump. Can you see them?"

Jess looked ahead and saw three low tree trunks lying in a row.

At Sarah's signal the ride began to gallop. Jess gathered up Storm Cloud's reins and nudged her forward, moving smoothly from a trot to a canter and then into a gallop. Three long strides and a signal from Jess, and Storm Cloud had cleared the first tree trunk, then the second and the third. It felt as if they were flying.

Jess brought Storm Cloud to a neat stop at the end of the field. Rosie drew up beside her, her cheeks flushed, and Pepper snorted heartily.

"You looked fantastic!" Rosie cried. "Storm Cloud jumps like a stag."

"She's amazing, isn't she?" replied Jess, with a happy sigh.

Chapter 9

Southdown at Last!

The next few days flew by. Before Jess knew it, Friday evening had arrived. Tomorrow was the Southdown Show.

Jess wandered restlessly around the house, unable to concentrate on anything or settle anywhere. She picked up the TV remote control and flipped through the channels but there was nothing she wanted to watch.

Maybe she was hungry. Jess padded into the kitchen and stood looking in the fridge.

"Close the door, Jess," said her dad. "You're letting

all the cold air out."

"What you need is a warm bath and an early night," her mother advised. "Stop worrying, Jess."

"I'm not worried," Jess said irritably. "Just excited."

Her mother smiled at her. Jess had been afraid her parents would disapprove of the horse show as it meant more time away from her school work, but they had been surprisingly encouraging.

"We'll be there to watch. We wouldn't miss it for the world," they had said.

Jess went to bed early that night. She didn't think she'd sleep at all, so she tried to fill her mind with pleasant thoughts of jumping ponies. The next thing she knew, daylight was streaming in through the curtains. It was Saturday and Southdown!

"We'll be by the ringside," her mother said at breakfast. "Now, are you sure you don't want a lift?"

Jess insisted she wanted to ride her bike to Sandy Lane.

"It's probably some sort of crazy good luck routine, Mom. I'd leave her to it," her brother Jack muttered.

Sandy Lane was buzzing with activity. The horse trailers stood ready for their precious cargo. Riders were scurrying about grooming, braiding manes, picking out hooves. Jess went to fling her bicycle down. Then she had second thoughts and leaned it carefully against the wall of the tack room. Alex and Kate called out to her. "We're your cheerleading team today. Good luck, Jess!"

Charlie was in Napoleon's stall, hurriedly brushing the horse's brown coat. "Perfect," he said, standing back to admire his work.

"You've missed a spot," Jess grinned, causing Charlie to inspect Napoleon for tiny specks of dirt.

She walked over to Minstrel, who was patiently peering over the stall door. The pony whinnied gently and his nostrils quivered with excitement.

"You know you're going to a show, boy, don't you?" Jess whispered in his ear. "Southdown Show, no less. You're going to be amazing."

CLANG!

Pepper's stall door swung open and Jess's peaceful

moment was interrupted by a clatter of hooves as the little pony jogged out of his stall, into the stable yard and off down the lane.

Rosie followed close behind. "He's spooking like crazy," she called over her shoulder.

She bolted after the little pony, but Pepper saw her coming and, with one effortless leap, he cleared the pond and landed in the grass on the other side. Unconcerned, he began to munch at the leaves on the overhanging trees. Twigs caught in his mane making a complete mess of the neat braids that had taken Rosie ages.

"Too bad, Rosie!" Charlie called.

When the ponies were almost ready, Nick called the team together.

"Trailer loading," he said. "You must all be responsible for getting your pony into the horse trailer as calmly as possible. So here's the order. Minstrel first, then Pepper in this trailer. Sarah will drive it. I'll be driving the other one with Napoleon, Feather and Storm Cloud."

"Storm Cloud?" Jess was immediately alert. "I didn't know she was coming. And Feather as well? Who'll be riding them, Nick?"

"Not so fast, Jess." Nick smiled. "Storm Cloud and Feather won't be entering any competitions today. But they'll be competing soon and they need to get used to a show atmosphere."

Jess looked sheepish at her eager outburst.

They loaded the horse trailers and were ready to go when a breathless voice made them all turn.

"Wait for me!" Belinda, dressed in pale beige jodhpurs and a dark jacket, climbed out of her mother's car and ran toward them.

"You came after all," Jess said.

"Well, there didn't seem much point moping around at home," Belinda explained with a smile.

"I need all the support I can get!" Jess grinned.

At last, they were off to Southdown and the show.

As they arrived, Jess felt a swirling mix of excitement and fear. Everywhere was bustling with activity. Show officials with loudspeakers and clipboards ran around, barking out instructions. Horse trailers of all shapes and sizes dotted the fields, each with horses and ponies in various states of grooming. A perfectly poised little girl on a tiny roan mare popped backwards and forwards over a practice jump. Riders in well-tailored black jackets and cream jodhpurs strode by confidently, greeting each other.

Over in the main field there were stalls and marquees selling everything from saddle soap to riding hats, hot dogs to barbecue sandwiches. Was it really only last year that she and Rosie had been here as enthralled spectators, the chances of them taking part only a dream? And now they were official competitors! They tethered the ponies and gave them a final grooming while Nick went off to check everyone in.

"I'll meet you by the ring," he called, "and we'll walk around the course together."

Jess struggled into her show jacket and turned to Rosie excitedly.

"Can you believe we're really here?" she breathed.

"I would be excited if I wasn't feeling so nervous," Rosie groaned in reply.

Jess looked around for Tom. She hadn't seen him since the day at the hospital. Would he be well enough to come?

At the show ring, Nick handed out their numbers then led them around the course. Belinda, Alex and Kate came too, for moral support. The fences looked big and Jess didn't like the look of the combination, but Nick had some words of advice.

"Keep the impulsion as you come around the corner and don't over ride it, Jess." Then he left for the competitors' tent.

"Have you jumped a course as hard as this, Belinda?" Jess asked.

"Um, no, actually." Belinda grinned. "It looks pretty challenging. You'll just have to take it steady and, well, enjoy it."

"Easier said than done." Jess groaned, but her insides had calmed down a little. She was almost looking forward to jumping. It was time to go and warm Minstrel up.

"I'll meet you back at the horse stalls," Belinda said. "I'm going to have a look at the dressage."

"And I promised to meet my mom by the officials' tent," Rosie called as Belinda went. "I won't be long."

Jess waved goodbye and followed Alex and Kate back to the stalls.

"Is Nick with you?" Sarah asked them.

"No, he's gone to the competitors' tent," said Alex.

"I'd better go and find him," said Sarah. "There's some man – says he knows Nick – who's asking to buy Storm Cloud. I said she wasn't for sale but he's very insistent. I need Nick to sort this one out. Will you keep an eye on the horses? Watch out for Pepper. He's been spooking a bit."

Buy Storm Cloud? Jess shook her head. Surely they would never sell her, but if this man was a friend of Nick's...

She went over to the gray mare, who stood grazing in the shade, ears alert to the sounds around her, her tail twitching nervously. As Jess approached, Storm Cloud lifted her head and whinnied. She nuzzled her soft nose into Jess's shoulder and her tail relaxed.

"Don't worry, Stormy," Jess whispered. "Nick and Sarah would never sell you. You're far too precious to them. And to me," she added, even more quietly.

Suddenly, a small brown dog tore around the corner of the stall yapping and snapping. Storm Cloud started but Jess laid a steadying hand on her neck and she was still again.

"Rags! Come back here," a child cried.

But Rags took no notice as he darted and weaved between the ponies' hooves.

Pepper shifted nervously and, at the small dog's shrill barking, he kicked out in a blind panic, hitting Minstrel on the fetlock. Minstrel whinnied in pain and reared up. When he landed, he began limping ominously.

Jess held onto Storm Cloud while Alex and Kate did their best to calm Minstrel and Pepper. Rags scampered off and his small owner finally caught up with him. But the damage had been done. Minstrel was limping badly. Nick and Sarah came running up. Jess knew from their faces that they had seen everything. It didn't look good.

"Oh no," Nick groaned as he carefully ran a hand down Minstrel's foreleg. "We'd better get the vet to look at this. I'm afraid you may not be riding Minstrel today, after all."

As Nick made his way to the secretary's tent, Jess stared in disbelief. This couldn't be happening. Poor Minstrel. Poor her! Was this the end of her Southdown dream?

Suddenly, her thoughts were disturbed by a breathless Belinda.

"Listen, oh listen, everyone."

"What's happened now?" sighed Sarah.

"I've seen her. She's here," Belinda gasped.

"Who's here?" Sarah asked.

"Golddust!" Belinda cried.

Chapter 10

Striking Gold

Golddust! Belinda's words were greeted with stunned silence. It was all too much to take in.

"Are you sure, Belinda?" Sarah asked.

"Of course I am," Belinda cried. "I'd recognize her anywhere." She stopped short as she saw the glum faces. "What's happened here?" she finished.

Jess found her voice and quickly explained about Minstrel's accident. Then Sarah took charge.

"Jess, I need to wait here for Nick," she said. "You go with Belinda and find out what's going on. But just remember to be very careful what you do and say – and come and get us if there are any problems."

Jess nodded and the two girls darted off through the crowds. The hustle and bustle only added to the confusion in Jess's head.

"Over here," said Belinda as she led the way to a small patch of trees. Jess squinted her eyes to get a better glimpse of the ponies. Blacks, bays, a roan and a gray. And suddenly she saw her, kicking her heels and dancing on the spot. A beautiful palomino pony with mane and tail the color of white gold and a small circle of white hair on her forehead.

"Golddust!" Belinda breathed.

"There's someone with her," Jess said, grabbing Belinda's arm.

A small girl with long braided hair was trying in vain to calm the jumpy pony. With every tug of the lead rope, Golddust became more frantic.

Belinda winced. "I can't stand it, Jess," she cried, and raced off toward Golddust, with Jess following close behind.

Belinda neared Golddust and slowed down. "It's

all right, girl, here I am," she assured the pony in low soothing tones.

At the sound of her voice, Golddust's ears twitched forward. Belinda laid a gentle hand across her neck. Golddust whinnied again, in sheer pleasure, and Belinda buried her head in the pony's mane.

"Thank you!" cried the girl hanging onto Golddust, sounding relieved.

Jess looked at the small upturned face streaked with sweat and tears.

"Are your parents here?" Jess asked kindly.

"Yes. They've left me looking after my sister's pony while they go to look at another one for her. This one's too much for her to handle."

"Has she had her long?" Jess asked.

"No, Daddy just bought her. Sorry, who are you? I'm not supposed to talk to strangers."

"I'm Jess and this is Belinda."

"I'm Sally," the girl replied, shyly. "My sister was supposed to be competing today, but this pony's practically wild."

"She isn't wild, she's just frightened," Belinda said lifting her head. "Where did you say your dad had bought her?"

"I don't know, I'm afraid. You'd need to ask him," Sally replied. "Why, what's wrong?"

"Sally," Jess said as gently as she could. "This pony is named Golddust. She belongs to Belinda. She was stolen from her a few weeks ago."

"Stolen!" Sally's eyes widened in disbelief. "But Daddy paid for her..."

"I'm sure he did," Belinda said quickly. "But she had already been stolen from me."

Sally fell into a stunned silence.

Jess shifted uncomfortably. "I think we ought to find your parents," she said quickly.

A look of relief spread across Sally's face. "Here they are now, with my sister."

Jess turned to follow Sally's eager gaze and gasped. The girl striding toward them was horribly familiar.

"Marissa Slater!" Jess cried.

"You!" Marissa sneered.

Behind her, talking in loud voices, strode Mr. Slater and a woman with the same disdainful expression as Marissa.

"What a shame Nick Brooks wouldn't sell that lovely gray pony. And after you rode her so well at Sandy Lane, pet," the woman trilled.

"I didn't want that pony anyway, Mother," Marissa hissed.

Jess couldn't believe her ears. They must be talking about Storm Cloud. But Marissa hadn't ridden her well at all, she had frightened poor Stormy half to death. What nerve – if only Marissa's mother knew the truth.

"Dad!" came Sally's anxious voice. "Marissa's pony has been stolen!"

"What are you talking about?" Marissa snorted. "She's right here."

"No," Sally cried. "I mean she's a stolen pony!"

"What nonsense," Mr. Slater boomed. "I paid the man with my own money."

"I'm sure you did," Belinda burst out. "But she's

really my pony and I can prove it. She's freezemarked right here." She pointed to a number on the little palomino's neck. "And I have all the documents at home."

Mrs. Slater looked furious. "I knew there was something fishy about the man you bought her from," she barked. "But you wouldn't listen to me, would you? You never do."

Mr. Slater looked harassed. "Oh no," he groaned. "But pet wanted that pony so badly. How was I to know..." He paused awkwardly.

"Let's go and get Nick," Jess said to Belinda.

"No!" Marissa spat.

Mr. Slater looked straight at Jess for the first time. "Don't I know you?" he asked.

"I took Marissa out for a ride at Sandy Lane," Jess admitted.

"Ah yes." Mr. Slater smiled affably. "Marissa told me how well she'd ridden. That's why we bought her a pony."

Jess shot Marissa a quick glance. Marissa cast her

eyes downwards and kicked at the grass with her heel. For a brief moment Jess considered telling Mr. Slater the truth about that day, but what was the point? Marissa obviously had him wrapped around her little finger. Anyway, there were more important things to sort out. Thankfully, Mr. Slater seemed to agree.

"Look, I'm going to get the police," he said. "I wouldn't want anyone to think I was a thief."

"Yes, I think you'd better," Mrs. Slater barked. "Just imagine what the neighbors would say!"

Jess smiled at Belinda, then looked at her watch in a panic. The junior jumping would be starting very soon.

"I have to get back to Minstrel," she cried.

"Of course." Belinda understood immediately. "Off you go, Jess. Everything is under control here."

And so Jess raced back to her Sandy Lane teammates, where she was greeted by a sea of glum faces. Rosie was the first to speak.

"It doesn't look good, Jess," she said. "The vet left

a while ago, and Nick and Sarah have been in a conspiratorial huddle for absolutely ages."

Jess groaned. Time was running out. Charlie was mounted and raring to go and Rosie was circling Pepper, warming the piebald up. They were low numbers, twelve and fourteen respectively, so they'd be jumping soon. Jess was number thirty-eight, second last, but she couldn't jump without Minstrel.

Finally, Nick and Sarah came over.

"It's bad news, I'm afraid, Jess," Nick said. "Minstrel's got a badly bruised left foreleg. He'll be all right, but there's no way he can jump today."

Jess lowered her head and tried to fight back the tears. To be given the chance to ride at Southdown and then to have it so cruelly snatched away from her at the last moment was almost more than she could bear.

Now Sarah was speaking but Jess wasn't taking anything in.

"Jess," Sarah repeated. "Didn't you hear me? You can ride Storm Cloud."

Jess was speechless.

"Only if you want to," Nick added. "She's an excellent jumper and you've ridden her well before. I'm not saying it will be easy, but if you take it steady I'm sure you'll be all right. So what do you say?"

What could she say? She was astounded that Nick and Sarah had that much faith in her. It was terrible that Minstrel was injured, but he would make a full recovery. And to ride Storm Cloud would be a dream come true.

"Oh thank you so much. Yes please!" Jess gasped.

Chapter 11

Showjumping

Storm Cloud stood steady and alert as Jess sprang lightly onto her back. She followed Rosie and Charlie to the collecting ring to warm up. Alex and Kate raced over, wanting to know why Jess was riding Storm Cloud. Jess hurriedly explained.

"Poor Minstrel. But how exciting for you," Kate exclaimed. "We've been watching the jumping so far. Some of the fences are really difficult."

"Well, jump five, the square vertical, seems to be causing problems," said Alex. "And judging the combination at the sixth looks tricky too."

At that moment, Jess's mom and dad appeared, smiling encouragingly. "You look very professional, Jess. Good luck!"

Jess beamed back at them.

"Competitor number ten," boomed the loudspeaker. "Belinda Lang on Golddust. This is a rider change."

What? Jess could hardly believe her ears. She quickly jumped down from Storm Cloud, tethered him at the stall and rushed over to watch Belinda and Golddust. She felt as nervous as if it were already her turn.

Golddust tossed her head playfully and held her magnificent tail up high as the sun glinted and danced on her golden coat. Belinda sat poised and calm, controlling Golddust with no perceptible movement. She caught Jess's eye and grinned wildly. Jess saw her confidence and began to relax. Watching Belinda would be a real treat.

With the ring of the bell, Golddust cantered off and all but flew over the bars then onto the brush and the gate. She made the difficult square vertical and the combination look easy. Even the triple bar, almost as tall as Golddust herself, was taken effortlessly, then it was the final wall and a roar from the crowd as they finished. Jess exhaled slowly.

"Clear round," boomed the loudspeaker.

"Wow, they were amazing!" said Rosie.

"She's good!" Alex said, approvingly.

"She'll be hard to beat," added Kate.

"Well, I'll give it a try." Charlie grinned.

Jess said nothing. She was thinking about how perfect Belinda and Golddust had looked together. As Belinda came up to them, Jess joined the others in congratulating her. She wanted to ask what had happened with the Slaters, but she knew now wasn't the time. Belinda was flushed with happiness.

"I would never have come to Southdown today if it hadn't been for you guys," she said. "And now I've found Golddust I feel like the luckiest person alive."

"Competitor number twelve. Charlie Marshall on Napoleon," came the announcement.

"Quick, we can't miss this," Kate said eagerly.

Charlie certainly cut an imposing figure as he rode Napoleon confidently into the ring.

"He's gorgeous," whispered a girl in front.

"The rider's not bad either," her friend replied.

Kate and Jess nudged each other and giggled. Soon they were lost in the swiftness and capability of Charlie's ride. And, before they knew it, he had ridden triumphantly out of the ring.

"Clear round!" the loudspeaker called.

"Oh no, it's me next," Rosie cried as competitor number thirteen sent the square vertical crashing to the ground. "Wish me luck," she called, riding away.

"You can do it, Rosie," Jess whispered fiercely.

Slowly, and with great determination, Rosie and Pepper cleared the ascending oxer and the bars. They clipped the top of the brush but the jump remained intact. Next it was the vertical, the combination, and finally the wall. They were over and clear. It wasn't fast, but it was effective. Pepper stalked out of the ring, tail held high.

"That was great, Rosie," Jess cried.

"I was a little slow." Rosie wrinkled her nose.

"But you jumped steadily and it was a clear round," Jess reassured her.

Nick joined their little group. "Well, I must say things are looking very good so far. Two clear rounds for Sandy Lane. And a clear for Belinda, our honorary member."

Belinda's eyes shone with delight at Nick's words. Jess smiled wanly. Would their good luck last? It was all up to her. Quietly she rode Storm Cloud away from the crowd and began her warm up. Round and round they walked in the practice field, every lap bringing them closer to their turn. At last competitor thirty-seven left the show ring, a trail of spectacular destruction in her wake.

"Sixteen faults for Amanda Matthews on Cinnamon," the loudspeaker confirmed.

"It's going to be a tough one, Storm Cloud," Jess murmured.

"You'll be fine, Jess."

A voice at her side made her jump in her saddle.

"Tom?" Jess gasped. "Oh you made it. Fantastic! How are you feeling?"

"Delicate," Tom smiled. "But excited too. I'm looking forward to seeing you jump. There have been eight clear rounds so far – yours will be the ninth." Jess's heart soared and suddenly she didn't feel so bad. If Tom thought she could do it...

"Thanks, Tom," she grinned.

"Competitor number thirty-eight, Jess Adams on Storm Cloud."

They trotted into the ring. Instantly Jess was nervous again. This was really it! She felt Storm Cloud quiver with anticipation and bent down to pat her dappled neck.

"We can do it, Stormy," she whispered.

She trotted Storm Cloud around the edge of the ring, battling hard to stop her nerves from interfering with her concentration. Suddenly the bell sounded.

As Jess cleared the first fence she felt a surge of confidence. The competition had begun! Now they were on course for the bars.

She urged Storm Cloud forward and kept her gaze firmly fixed between Storm Cloud's alert ears. The spirited pony knew exactly what was needed and soared through the air, leaving inches of space between herself and the jump.

Onwards they rode, up and over the brush and towards the gate. Storm Cloud reached high for the obstacle and cleared it, but she overbalanced on landing and Jess was flung forward.

Swiftly Jess tried to right herself as she turned Storm Cloud in the approach to the vertical, but she was losing contact. Storm Cloud sensed Jess's dilemma and knew what was expected of her. Valiantly she attempted the jump. As the pony's head came up, Jess was struck on the chin. She bit her lip heavily and tasted blood, then heard Storm Cloud's hind legs rap the top pole.

Jess regained her balance and cantered on, all the time straining to hear the thud of pole hitting grass. She couldn't look back, but the gasp of relief from the crowd told her the pole had stayed in place.

Whew!

"Nice work, Storm Cloud," she breathed. "I won't make that mistake again!"

With renewed confidence, she rode Storm Cloud straight and square toward the combination. Storm Cloud flicked her tail and thundered on.

"Steady, steady," Jess chanted under her breath.

One, two, three, jump! And they were over the first combination. Storm Cloud flew through the air. Touchdown! Take off! And they were soaring again. Clear and away. They flew over the cross poles and jumped the wall with ease, then they were finished and out of the ring.

"We did it," she cried, flinging her arms around the pony's neck.

"Clear round for competitor thirty-eight, Jess Adams on Storm Cloud," confirmed the loudspeaker.

Everyone gathered around to congratulate her.

"Amazing, Jess," said Nick, giving Storm Cloud a pat. "You rode very well."

Jess glowed with happiness and pride. But it wasn't over yet. She was through to the jump-off – against the clock this time.

She led Storm Cloud to cool down beneath the trees before their big moment arrived and tried to focus on how to get the best performance out of Storm Cloud.

There were ten riders in all for the final competition. Jess was jumping fifth, Belinda ninth, Charlie seventh and poor Rosie first. As much as Jess wanted to cheer on the others, she couldn't bear to watch.

When her number was called, she had no idea what time she had to beat. She would just have to jump the round of her life.

"This is it, girl," Jess whispered, as Storm Cloud skipped and danced beneath her.

"Good luck, Jess," she heard Tom call.

Storm Cloud tossed her smoke-gray mane and trotted once again into the ring.

"Relax, relax," Jess whispered, as they circled.

The bell rang and they were off! Swift and steady to the first jump. A light tap of her heels and Storm Cloud was over and riding squarely for the bars. Up and away and they were down again. Jess felt as light as a feather.

Turning nimbly, she headed Storm Cloud for the brush, counting the strides with every thunder of Storm Cloud's hooves. One and two and three and they were over. Then they had cleared the gate before Jess had time to catch her breath.

This time, Jess was ready for the vertical. She checked Storm Cloud and set her square. Jess felt Storm Cloud's front legs tuck well underneath her as she sprang high into the air and over the pole. Clear! Next it was the combination, a tight turn, the triple bar and finally the wall. Storm Cloud took them all in her stride.

"Fantastic!" Jess cried, clasping her arms around Storm Cloud's warm neck.

"Jess Adams, clear in fifty-three seconds," the loudspeaker boomed.

Jess was exhilarated. It sounded fast, but was it fast enough?

"Great job, Jess!" Nick called. "You really got the best out of Storm Cloud."

"Oh, Jess, that was amazing," Rosie cried as she rushed up. "You did miles better than me. Pepper clipped the wall with his heels. That's four faults automatically."

Alex grinned wildly at her. "That was some performance, Jess. I think you're in with a chance of a ribbon. Nice job."

Jess shook her head. "It was Storm Cloud, not me," she protested.

The next competitor crashed into the brush and netted herself four faults.

And then it was Charlie's turn. Jess had to admit they looked magnificent. Napoleon's healthy brown coat shone in the bright sunlight and Charlie pressed him on over the jumps. This time he must have remembered Nick's advice. He didn't rush the course but took it steadily and swiftly.

"Charlie Marshall on Napoleon, jumping clear in forty-nine seconds," echoed the speaker.

"He was fantastic," Jess said.

"He's in the lead," Rosie shouted at Jess's side.

The next rider did well too.

"Melissa James, jumping clear in fifty-one seconds," declared the loudspeaker.

"Not as fast as Charlie," Alex muttered.

"But faster than me," Jess noted, and realized she didn't mind. She had done her best and she was happy. Now it was time to watch Belinda.

Jess gazed in awe as Belinda cantered Golddust easily around the ring. She was enthralled by Belinda's performance. Swiftly and efficiently Golddust cleared the jumps, and at what a pace.

"Clear in forty-six seconds," the announcement came. "Belinda Lang takes the lead on Golddust."

The final competitor failed to beat Belinda's time and that made her the winner.

Jess smiled in admiration. She knew she and Storm Cloud had jumped superbly but it was Belinda who had been the best and truly deserved to win.

"Come on," Rosie urged, tugging Jess's sleeve.

"What's the hurry?" Jess asked in surprise. She didn't want to leave just yet.

"We've got to go into the ring to receive our prizes," said Rosie.

"Prizes?" Jess was confused.

"You came fourth, silly," Rosie laughed. "And I was sixth. We're winners at Southdown!"

Jess could hardly believe it. She climbed into Storm Cloud's saddle and rode into the ring.

"Get behind me, Jess." Charlie grinned. "I came second, you know."

Jess saw her parents, grinning with pride. Tom was there too, and Alex and Kate, cheering and clapping.

Jess's heart jumped as she caught a glimpse of Marissa and Sally watching them closely.

In the background, Nick and Sarah were talking urgently to Mr. Slater and a policeman. But nothing else mattered to Jess now.

As she followed Charlie into the ring for the celebratory lap of honor she could only sit up straight, and beam and beam.

Chapter 12

Runaway Returns

"I can't believe Mr. Slater gave Golddust back so easily," said Rosie.

Jess and Rosie were sitting in the tack room at Sandy Lane on the Saturday after the Southdown Show. A tin of saddle soap stood open on the table in front of them and they were polishing their way through a jumble of stirrup leathers.

"What could he do?" said Jess. "Because Golddust was stolen, the police said she still belonged to the original owner. That didn't stop Marissa from being furious about Belinda riding her though!"

So far the police hadn't managed to track down the man who sold Golddust to the Slaters, but they hadn't given up hope of catching him. Golddust was back with Belinda, and Nick and Sarah had offered Belinda temporary use of the spare loose stall at Sandy Lane. With a thief still around, Belinda couldn't be careful enough.

"Who am I booked on for the 11 o'clock ride?" asked Alex, striding in to join Rosie and Jess in the tack room.

"Hello, Alex. You're on Hector, I think," Jess said.

"What, that lumbering old thing?" Alex groaned, but he was only joking. Alex loved Hector and Jess and Rosie knew it.

"Who's a lumbering old thing?" a familiar, friendly voice inquired.

"Tom!" Jess and Rosie exclaimed together. "You're back. Are you riding today? Are you feeling better? Have you missed Chancey?"

"Woah, ease off with the questions," he grinned. "Let me see. No, I'm not riding today. I'm not quite up to that yet, although yes I am feeling better. And yes, of course I've missed Chancey."

"Hey, everyone," Charlie squeezed in. "Who am I riding then?"

But no one had time to answer him as an angry Kate appeared at the doorway, hands on hips.

"Okay, Alex, that's it," she said, her eyes glinting furiously. "Just because your bike's got a flat, it doesn't give you the right to take mine."

"Sorry, Kate." Alex shrank guiltily into a corner. "But you took so long getting ready this morning, and your bike was just sitting there looking all shiny and tempting and..."

"Hello, everybody." Belinda appeared. "I've come to take Golddust out. How's Minstrel today, Jess?"

"He's much better, thanks," Jess replied. "I'm riding him later."

Then Nick popped his head around the tack room door. "There's someone asking for you outside, Jess."

"It's Marissa Slater. She wants a private lesson," said Charlie, teasingly.

By now everyone at Sandy Lane knew the Marissa story. Jess wasn't amused. She glared at him as she walked out. Blinking in the bright sunshine, Jess found herself face to face with a stocky man. It was Bob Hughes.

"I've brought Goldie and Mary to see you," he announced.

Sure enough, beside him was Mary on top of a beautiful palomino pony.

"Goldie," Jess breathed. "And Mary! You look so much better. Can I pet your pony?"

"Of course." Mary smiled down at Jess. "It's my first ride since I got out of the hospital," she explained. "We just live up the Ash Hill road so we thought we'd stop in and say hello."

"I'm glad you've come," Jess said. "That's Belinda's pony, Golddust, over there," she said, pointing. "She's the one I confused Goldie with, although they don't actually look that similar, do they?"

Mary smiled and at that moment, Belinda came out of the tack room.

"Is this the runaway palomino pony?" she asked.

"Yes," said Jess. "Funny to see both Goldie and Golddust together."

"Mary!" Tom's voice called from the tack room door. "How are you feeling?"

"Hello, Tom," Mary replied as she slipped down from the saddle. "OK-ish. You're looking well."

"Thanks, I'm feeling it too."

"What a beautiful pony." Rosie, Charlie, Alex and Kate crowded eagerly around Mary. Goldie jumped back in startled surprise at all this attention and moved closer to Golddust. The two ponies neighed gently at each other and stood nose to nose, breathing softly.

Jess stood back a little way from her friends and watched them all, eagerly chatting and laughing. *How lucky we are*, she thought.

From the stall behind her came a soft whinny. Storm Cloud was hanging her head over her door as usual, her delicate gray face turned toward Jess.

Jess walked slowly toward her and breathed

softly into the little pony's nose.

"I haven't forgotten you, Stormy," she whispered. "We'll ride again soon. Nick promised we could."

"Come on, Jess," interrupted Rosie, cheerfully. "It's nearly 11 o'clock. Minstrel and Pepper are waiting. Let's go and tack up."